Dear mouse friends,
Welcome to the world of

Geronimo Stilton

MINI MYSTERY
3

THE RODENT'S GAZETTE
EDITORIAL STAFF

Geronimo Stilton
A learned and brainy
mouse; editor of
The Rodent's Gazette

Thea Stilton
Geronimo's sister and
special correspondent at
The Rodent's Gazette

Trap Stilton
An awful joker;
Geronimo's cousin and
owner of the store
Cheap Junk for Less

Benjamin Stilton
A sweet and loving
nine-year-old mouse;
Geronimo's favorite
nephew

Geronimo Stilton

THE MOUSE HOAX

Scholastic Inc.

ISBN 978-0-545-10373-2

Based on an original idea by Elisabetta Dami.
www.geronimostilton.com

Published by Scholastic Inc., 557 Broadway, New York, NY 10012.
SCHOLASTIC and associated logos are trademarks and/or registered trademarks of Scholastic Inc.

Stilton is the name of a famous English cheese. It is a registered trademark of the Stilton Cheese Makers' Association. For more information, go to www.stiltoncheese.com.

Text by Geronimo Stilton
Original title *Il topo falsario*
Cover by Giuseppe Ferrario
Illustrations by Claudio Cernuschi
Color by Giuseppe Di Dio
Graphics by Michela Battaglin

Special thanks to AnnMarie Anderson
Translated by Julia Heim
Interior design by Becky James

Fingerprint on cover and page i © NREY/Shutterstock

12 11 10 9 8 7 6 5 4 3 2 1   12 13 14 15 16 17/0

Printed in the U.S.A.   132
First printing, November 2012

A STRANGE LITTLE GIFT

It was a busy day at the office. The telephones wouldn't stop ringing!

"Hello?" I answered my **desk phone**.

"Mr. Stilton? It's Mitzy Mouserson. Remember me?"

"Yes?" I answered my **cell phone**.

"Stilton, it's Andrew Whitetail. About that manuscript . . ."

On top of the phone calls, every few minutes someone entered my office and I lost my TRAIN of thought. Oh, excuse me! I haven't introduced myself. My name is Stilton, *Geronimo Stilton*, and I am the publisher of *The Rodent's Gazette*, the most **famouse** newspaper on Mouse Island.

So, I was in my office when an **enoRMouSe** package entered the room. A familiar snout poked out from behind it.

"**Happy birthday**, Stilton!" a voice shouted.

It was my friend Hercule Poirat, the famouse detective.

"Birthday?" I repeated. "But TODAY isn't my birthday!"

"Oh, well," Hercule replied as he placed the package on my desk. "You should take the day off anyway!"

"Oh, I can't," I told him. "I have a **LOT** to do today."

Hercule got closer to my desk.

"Yes, I see that," he said. "You're always here, working. You should get out more! A change would be good for you. Come with me to my office."

My whiskers trembled at just the thought of the flea-infested shack Hercule calls his office. He is a complete slob, and his office is a total disaster area!

"I'm sorry, I can't," I told him quickly. "I really have to finish this article."

Hercule sighed. "All right, Stilton. I'll go. But first open the little gift I got you. Aren't you even a little curious about what's inside?"

A REAL STINKER

Inside the package was a painting. It was no masterpiece. In fact, it looked like it had been painted by my little cousin **MESSY PAWS**, and he's just a baby! It was a real **stinker**!

In the lower right-hand corner were the painter's initials: P.M.

"Do you like it?" Hercule asked me.

"Er, yes, of course!" I replied. I didn't want to offend him. "But it's a bit . . . odd. Where did you get it?"

"A while ago, I met a rat who was down on his **luck**," Hercule replied. "He gave it to me in exchange for some **BREAD** and **cheese**. Isn't it great?"

At that moment, one of the new editors, **Katie Cheeseheart**, popped in.

"Are you ready for the **ART EXHIBIT**?" she asked. "Tonight is the opening, **remember**?"

THE INVITATION
TO THE SHOW

Oh, for the love of cheese! I had completely forgotten about the art show opening of the great painter PABLO MOUSEHASSO.

"Petunia Pretty Paws called," Katie told me. "She and Bugsy Wugsy will be there."

Ah, Petunia Pretty Paws! She is the most fascinating rodent I know. I have a TEENY, tiny crush on her.

"You can bring guests," Katie reminded me.

"I'll come!" Hercule said eagerly.

I sighed. Hercule is a very **good** friend, but whenever he's around, I end up in a **SEA** of trouble.

"Well, er, actually . . . I promised Benjamin I would take him," I replied.

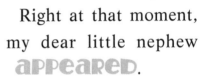

Right at that moment, my dear little nephew **appeared**.

"Hi, **BENJAMIN**!" I exclaimed.

"Hi, Uncle G!" Benjamin said as he gave me a **huge** hug. "Is Hercule coming with us to the show? How nice!"

Hercule **winked** at me, and we all left together.

A RATASTIC VILLA!

The show was in Master Mousehasso's house.

"This guy sure has a **ratastic** villa!" exclaimed Hercule.

"**Shhhhh!**" I quieted him. "Do you want them to kick us out?"

At that moment, I heard the *sweetest* voice behind me.

"Hi, G!"

It was Petunia Pretty Paws!

Then a little mouse with black **braids** jumped out at me and threw her arms around my neck — it was Bugsy, Petunia's

niece and Benjamin's **best friend**.

I let the ladies enter first and then I gave the *invitations* to the butler.

"Mr. Stilton!" the butler exclaimed. "What an HONOR. And are these other guests with you?"

"Yes, this is my **nephew** Benjamin," I replied. "And this, er, is the famouse investigator Hercule Poirat."

Hercule was busy WAVING his magnifying glass in the butler's face.

My snout turned **purple** with embarrassment, but the butler didn't TWITCH a whisker.

"Welcome," he said kindly. "Please CLIMB this main stairway. On the

second floor you will see the BUFFET.
Have a good evening!"

"Thank you!" I replied, trying to smile
through my embarrassment.

Hercule disappeared in the crowd.

I offered my arm to **Petunia**, and we climbed the main stairway that led to the second floor.

I was on cloud nine!

THE GREAT
MOUSEHASSO

The main hall was full of people admiring the paintings that hung on the walls. In one corner, I saw a rodent surrounded by photographers and admirers. It was Master Mousehasso!

"I want to see if I can get a picture, too!" Bugsy said as she showed off her digital camera with pride. "Come with me, Benjamin!"

"Can I, Uncle G?" Benjamin squeaked.

"Of course, Benjamin!" I said.

I was finally alone with Petunia when Hercule suddenly appeared, speaking

loudly as he was snacking.

"But . . . *chomp* . . . that guy . . . *chomp, chomp* . . . I . . . *chomp* . . ."

"Hercule!" I scolded. "You shouldn't talk with your mouth **fULL**!"

He just laughed.

"While you fill your head with art, I fill my stomach with food!"

My snout turned **purple** with embarrassment.

He ignored me.

"Listen up, Stilton," Hercule *whispered*. "This Mousehasso guy — I've seen him before, but I can't *remember* where. I just might go over there and ask him."

And he **disappeared** again!

Petunia turned to me and smiled *sweetly*.

"Why don't we go and get something to eat?" she asked.

So we approached the **super-crowded** refreshment table.

I had just managed to get my paws on two Gorgonzola **tarts** when a rodent asked: "Do you like my work?"

TARTS AND
COUNTESSES

The rodent stuck out his PAW.

"It's very nice to meet you," he said. "I am Master PABLO MOUSEHASSO."

"M-my name is Stilton, *Geronimo Stilton*," I stuttered. I could hardly believe I was speaking with a master artist! "I am —"

"Oh, I know who you are!" he replied with a smile. "And I want to offer you an exclusive **interview** for your newspaper. What do you say?"

"That sounds FABUMOUSE!" I exclaimed. "When can we do it?"

"Right away!" he said. "Just follow me into my studio. Naturally, your LOVELY girlfriend can come with us!"

My snout turned **purple** with embarrassment. I haven't yet had the courage to tell Petunia how I feel about her!

"Can our niece and nephew come, too?" Petunia asked.

"It would be a **pleasure** to meet them," Mousehasso replied.

Meanwhile, Hercule was approaching. I didn't want him to see us: Who knew what kind of mess Hercule would get me into!

I turned red . . .

But right as he was arriving, Mousehasso **mumbled** something and ran off.

"Taste this!" Hercule said as he shoved a tart into my mouth. The TART went down the wrong pipe, and I turned **RED**, then green, then as

. . . then green . . .

. . . then as white as mozzarella!

WHITE as mozzarella.

Hercule **HIT** me really hard on the back until I spit out the tart. It flew across the room, hitting Countess Snobella in the back of the neck.

"How rude!" she shrieked, smacking me with a **CANE**.

"Oh, for the love of bananas!"

Hercule shouted. "Stilton, when will you learn to leave little *old* ladies alone?"

When she heard Hercule call her an old lady, Countess Snobella began **CHASING** after him instead. I sighed with **relief** and led Petunia out of the way.

An Exclusive Interview

The butler approached me.

"Mr. Stilton, the **MASTER** is waiting for you," he said.

I called Benjamin and Bugsy Wugsy, and together we all went into the studio.

"Shall we begin?" the **artist** asked. "I only have a few minutes."

"Yes, of course," I replied. "So, how did you become such a success?"

"It wasn't easy," Master Mousehasso said. "In the beginning, I never had much money or enough to eat. Sometimes I had to give away my paintings in exchange

for a bit of **BREAD** and **cheese**!"

How strange! That sentence sounded very familiar.

Mousehasso continued. "Because I remember my humble beginnings, I am organizing a charity **auction** of a few of my works the day after tomorrow. The proceeds will help young artists. I hope you can make it."

"Oh, yes," I replied. "It would be a great HONOR."

Master Mousehasso rang a bell, and the butler

appeared with two ENORMOUSE packages.

Mousehasso gave one to Petunia and one to me.

"Don't open them right away," he instructed us. "It's a surprise!"

"I don't know how to thank you," I said breathlessly.

"Oh, it's nothing!" he replied. "I look forward to seeing you at the auction."

What a scoop!

I couldn't wait to get back to my office to write my article.

CLUE 1

Why did Master Mousehasso's sentence seem familiar to Geronimo?

THE MASTER'S GIFT

The next day, copies of *The Rodent's Gazette* flew off the stands. Bugsy's **photos** came out so well that I published one on the front page.

As I was enjoying my success, the phone rang.

It was Petunia Pretty Paws.

"Hi, G," she said sweetly. "There's a beautiful horse **GALLOPING** in my painting. What's yours like?"

For the love of cheese! I hadn't opened my gift from the master yet!

"I'll look right now," I told Petunia.

I would have preferred to paint it in your office, but I wanted to surprise you!

Pablo Mousehasso

To:
Geronimo Stilton

Then I opened the package.

For the love of cheese! It was me!

"So, G?" Petunia asked. "What is it?"

My snout turned **purple** with embarrassment. It's a good thing Petunia couldn't see me.

"Er, well . . . it's a portrait of me," I replied.

"Really?" Petunia asked. "I'll come right over so I can see it. You don't mind, do you?"

Mind? I was on cloud nine!

I hung the PAINTING facing my desk, right next to the painting Hercule had given me.

Now this is a real masterpiece, I thought. *It's nothing like that* stinker!

Then the door to my office suddenly BURST open.

PABLO MOUSEHASSO

BREAD AND CHEESE

It was **Hercule Poirat**!

"Stilton!" he exclaimed. "I remembered where I've seen Mousehasso before! He was the rat who gave me the painting in exchange for some BREAD and cheese! He was such a TERRIBLE artist I don't know how he ever got famous!"

"Well, he isn't TERRIBLE anymore," I said. "Look what he gave me."

I pointed to the portrait hanging on the wall.

Hercule approached it with his magnifying glass.

"You put it right next to the stinker!" he exclaimed. "Didn't you notice anything STRANGE about these two paintings?"

Hercule was right — how had I missed it?

CLUE 2

What did Hercule Poirat notice about the two paintings?

ARE YOU OKAY, G?

"The same mouse couldn't have painted **both** of these," I squeaked.

"It's quite a mystery," Hercule agreed.

At that moment, Bugsy, Benjamin, and Petunia Pretty Paws came in.

"Are you okay, G?" Petunia asked.

"I just made an important discovery," I told her. "LOOK! The SIGNATURES are similar. The initials in the corner of the painting Hercule gave me are the same as Pablo Mousehasso's!"

"Hey, *I* made the DISCOVERY!"

Hercule protested.

Bugsy picked up a slip of paper from the **ground** and handed it to me.

"This fell," she said.

"Thanks," I replied. It was the master's NOTE to me.

"**MOLDY MOZZARELLA!**" I exclaimed in surprise. "Look at this **strange** writing on the back of the note!"

I held it out for my friends to see.

YBU HTE
CLBAK
LTESRTE

THE ANAGRAM

"What does it mean?" Hercule asked.

"It's an ANAGRAM!" Petunia exclaimed.

"A **telegram**?" Hercule replied.

"No, an anagram." I explained, "It's a game in which the letters of a word are scrambled and need to be put back in order."

"Let's figure it out!"

Bugsy said. "The first group of letters is
YBU. What does that mean?"

I thought and thought.

"Um, UBY?" I suggested. "YUB?"

"I'VE GOT IT!" Hercule shouted.
"It spells BUY!"

"Nice work!" Benjamin and Bugsy
exclaimed in unison. "Now we need
to do the same thing with the other
groups of letters to make a sentence."

CLUE 3

Try to solve the anagram.
What sentence do you get?

THE CODED MESSAGE

I was PERPLEXED. "What does 'buy the black letters' mean?"

"I don't think this sentence was written by the master," Benjamin pointed out. "The handwriting looks different."

"So someone else knew about the gift Master Mousehasso gave Uncle G," observed Bugsy. "And that mouse wrote a coded message to let Uncle G know —"

"To buy the black letters!" Benjamin finished with **excitement**.

"They must be for sale if Geronimo is supposed to buy them," Hercule **muttered**. "But who would be selling **BLACK LETTERS**?"

"I know!" exclaimed Petunia. "Tomorrow **morning** is Mousehasso's charity auction at his villa."

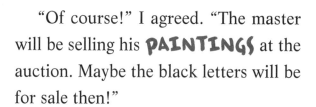

"Of course!" I agreed. "The master will be selling his **PAINTINGS** at the auction. Maybe the black letters will be for sale then!"

THE CHARITY AUCTION

When we arrived at the charity auction at Pablo Mousehasso's villa the next morning, the butler handed us a **catalog** of all the paintings that were for sale. Then we walked around to take a **look** at them.

"If you notice anything **strange**, let me know!" Hercule told us.

We stopped in front of a painting of a lake surrounded by **snowcapped** mountains.

"Do you see anything odd in this painting?" Bugsy Wugsy asked Hercule.

"Well, now that you mention it, yes I do," Hercule replied. "Those clouds remind me of a banana smoothie, and those mountains look a little like banana cakes!"

I rolled my eyes. Hercule LOVES

bananas the way most mice love cheese.

"Hey!" Benjamin whispered. "I see something strange. Look in the bottom right corner!"

"But of course!" Hercule exclaimed LOUDLY.

I didn't know what they were talking about. I didn't see anything but Master Mousehasso's SIGNATURE. But then I looked more closely.

BUT OF COURSE!

CLUE 4

What did Benjamin see in the painting?

THE BLACK LETTERS

There was a black letter in the white signature! It had to be one of the **BLACK LETTERS**. But where were the others?

We didn't have time to look because the auction was about to **start**.

"*Psst,*" Hercule whispered. "Let's

look in the catalog and find the paintings with **BLACK** letters. WE'LL BUY ALL OF THEM!"

Finding the paintings was easy: There were five of them!

"Soon we'll know what the author of the MYSTERIOUS note wanted to say!" Petunia said.

I had a sudden realization. "Who is going to PAY for all of these paintings?"

Benjamin gave me a pleading look.

"Won't **you**, Uncle?"

I could never say no to my **sweet** little nephew!

"Of course, Benjamin," I told him. "After all, there's a mystery to solve!"

Landscape
40" x 27"

Lower left:
Still Life of Fruit and Cheese
20" x 35"

Lower right
Mousilda
27" x 43"

Light and Sea
50" x 25"

Red Flowers
50" x 25"

START YOUR BIDDING!

"Do you want some help bidding, Stilton?" Hercule asked.

"Oh, no!" I said.

"It's no problem," he replied. "I'll just offer an amount that's a little **TOO HIGH** to make sure we get the painting!"

"**Absolutely not!**" I insisted, twisting my whiskers anxiously. "I'll go **broke**!"

"Oh, fine." Hercule pouted. "Do it your way!"

The first few **PAINTINGS** were not the ones with the black letters. We watched the other rodents bid.

Holey cheese! The prices were so high I almost fainted.

"Why are they raising their paws, Uncle?" Benjamin asked.

"To show the price they are willing to pay," I replied. "Each raised paw means they are willing to pay **fifty dollars** more

than the previous rodent."

"**WOW!**" Benjamin exclaimed. "Those are some expensive paintings!"

Finally, the painting with the banana cake–shaped mountains came up.

"The opening price for this *splendid* painting is five hundred dollars," the auctioneer said. "Ladies and gentlemice, start your bidding!"

Five hundred dollars! I was about to faint from the price, but I raised my paw anyway.

"Five hundred **DOLLARS** to the

gentlemouse in the back!"

A lady rodent in the first row raised her hand.

"Five hundred fifty **DOLLARS** to the lady in front!"

Several more rodents raised their paws. Suddenly, a waiter came in with a huge tray of banana cream pastries.

Hercule waved his arms to get the waiter's attention: He really LOVES bananas! But every time he raised his arm, the auctioneer raised the price!

I tried to stop him, but Hercule continued lifting his arms until, finally, we got the painting for . . .

ONE THOUSAND DOLLARS!

ASTRONOMICAL PRICES

We still needed to buy **four** more paintings. And every time a **waiter** passed by with a tray of treats, Hercule raised his arm, **increasing** the price!

During bidding for the second painting, there was a tray of banana **muffins**.

I was going broke!

During bidding for the third painting, Hercule waved for the crispy banana chips.

SECOND PAINTING

THIRD PAINTING

FOURTH PAINTING

FIFTH PAINTING

I was really going broke!

During bidding for the fourth painting, the tray was full of banana sundaes.

I was really, really going broke!

During bidding for the fifth painting, I gave up.

I was completely broke!

But I was happy anyway. After all, the money was for a good cause!

ANOTHER ANAGRAM

After the auction, we RETURNED to my house to study the **FIVE** paintings.

"So? Have you *discovered* anything?" asked Petunia.

"Well, the black letters are **L**, **M**, **E**, **H**, **P**, and **E**," Hercule replied.

"We knew that just by looking at the catalog!" said Benjamin.

"Yes, but we hadn't figured out that it was another kilogram!" explained Hercule.

"You mean another ANAGRAM," I told Hercule. "What do the letters spell?"

"Let's try rearranging them a few different ways," Benjamin suggested.

"H-E-E-L-M-P?" I suggested.

"M-E-E-P-H-L?" Bugsy tried.

HELP ME!

Hercule **nibbled** his way through five bananas and drank **two** banana smoothies as we worked.

"Maybe it's two words," Benjamin said. "Otherwise there are a lot of consonants."

"I figured it out!" Hercule shouted. "The letters spell **HELP ME**!"

"'Help me'?" I asked in astonishment. "Someone must be in **trouble**!"

"Who could it be?" asked Bugsy.

Hercule was so excited that he accidentally spilled his smoothie on one of the paintings. The paint smeared as he wiped it off.

"Look at this!" exclaimed Petunia.

A hidden picture had appeared.

"It's part of a **MAP**!" Bugsy realized. "But it's incomplete."

"I think I know where the rest of the map is," said Benjamin. "Hercule, can you wipe off the other paintings?"

THE MAP

Hercule didn't need to be asked twice: He happily spilled the smoothie on all the paintings to reveal the pieces of the map. One of the paintings, however, didn't seem to have a part of the map. How strange!

Hercule inspected every inch of the canvas until he discovered an eight-digit number in the corner.

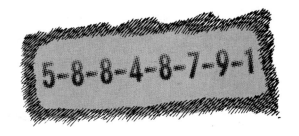

"What do these numbers mean?" Petunia asked.

"**I don't know**, but we'll figure it out!" Benjamin replied.

Meanwhile, Hercule put all the pieces of the map **TOGETHER**. The map's shape looked very familiar. I felt as though I had been to the place in the drawing. But **WHERE** was it?

Suddenly, Bugsy and **BENJAMIN**

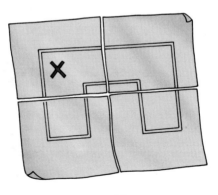

exclaimed in unison: **"We've got it!"**

"By my banana, I've got it, too!" Hercule cried.

"Me, too!" added Petunia. "You recognize it, don't you, G?"

Suddenly, it came to me.

BUT OF COURSE!

CLUE 5

Do you recognize the place drawn on the map?

THE LAST PIECE
OF THE PUZZLE

The mystery location on the map was Pablo Mousehasso's very own villa!

"WE DON'T HAVE A MINUTE TO SPARE!" Hercule exclaimed.

We hurried outside to a **TAXI**.

When we arrived at the villa, the

butler opened the door.

"The master is not at home," he told us. "He's at a ceremony receiving the RODENT OF THE YEAR award."

"That's perfect," I said. "We aren't here to see him anyway."

"Let's hurry!" Benjamin said as he slipped past the butler.

"Hey, wait a minute," protested the butler. "You can't just come in here!"

"You have to let us in," Bugsy insisted. "Someone's in trouble!"

The butler didn't know what to say. We just walked by him into the villa. Then we used the MAP to find the spot that was marked with an X.

We ended up in a small **STORAGE ROOM** in the cellar.

"Look, there's a **little door** down there!" exclaimed Bugsy.

We opened the door and found ourselves in front of a **WALL** made of bricks, some with markings numbering

them from **one** to **nine**.

Oh, for the love of cheese! We were so close to solving the mystery, but the wall was **blocking** us.

"I've got it!" Benjamin exclaimed suddenly. He PULLED the piece of canvas with the eight numbers from his pocket. Then he **pushed** on different bricks. The wall moved to reveal a secret passage. A small, skinny rodent appeared before our **eyes**.

"Finally you're here!" he said.

CLUE 6

How was Benjamin able to open the door to the secret passage?

SALVADOR RATI

The rodent explained the whole story.

"My name is Salvador Rati," he told us. "I met Pablo Mousehasso many years ago, when he was KICKED OUT

of the New Mouse City art school. He was a charming mouse, but he didn't know what to do with a PAINTBRUSH between his paws! I, on the other hand, was talented but very shy. So he made me a proposal: I would create paintings that he would sign and sell, and we would split the profits."

"What a **cheater**!" Hercule exclaimed.

"My **PAINTINGS** did very well," Rati continued, "but Mousehasso was the one becoming FAMOUSE. He kept asking for more and more of the money. When I told him that I was tired of the lie, he locked me in his villa and forced me to work for **FREE**."

"That's awful!" Benjamin exclaimed.

The rest of us nodded in agreement.

"It's time to expose this **HOAX**," Hercule announced. "And I have a plan!"

RODENT OF THE YEAR

We arrived just in time at the theater where the RODENT OF THE YEAR awards ceremony was being held. The presentation had already begun.

Hercule disappeared backstage with Rati while the rest of us sat in the last row.

"And now, the moment you've all been waiting for: the RODENT OF THE YEAR award!" the emcee announced.

The **hostess** turned over the envelope.

"The most important rodent in New Mouse City this year is . . . **Salvador Rati**?!"

A **murmur** spread through the room.

I don't know how Hercule had done it, but he had managed to change the winner's name at the last **minute**!

Pablo Mousehasso stormed onstage, as **RED** as a tomato.

"Who dares to steal my *prize*?" he bellowed.

"I do!" Rati announced as he stepped onto the stage as well.

Mousehasso gasped.

"How did you manage to *escape*?" he asked. "Uh, I mean . . . who are you?"

"I'm a real **PAINTER**, not a con artist like you!" Rati said proudly.

"**THAT'S NOT TRUE!**" Mousehasso replied. "I'm a great painter!"

"Then prove it," Rati said calmly. "Right now, in front of everyone. You will **paint** my portrait, and I will **paint** yours!"

Mousehasso turned as pale as a slice of mozzarella, but there was no way around it. He had to agree to the challenge!

Rati, on the other paw, seemed very sure of himself as the emcee set up two easels and two canvases on the stage.

With trembling paws, Mousehasso began to paint. The crowd murmured softly.

This was the result:

PORTRAIT OF SALVADOR RATI
PAINTED BY PABLO MOUSEHASSO

Then it was Rati's turn. He picked up a brush and in a flash painted a *splendid* portrait of Mousehasso. The crowd broke out in **applause**.

PORTRAIT OF PABLO MOUSEHASSO
PAINTED BY SALVADOR RATI

THE TRUE STORY OF SALVADOR RATI

Salvador Rati was given the RODENT OF THE YEAR award, and Pablo Mousehasso went to jail, where he began taking a painting class.

The Rodent's Gazette published an exclusive story about Salvador Rati, and it was an enormouse success!

To celebrate, I invited all my friends to my house for a party. Rati was the guest of honor.

It was an unforgettable night!

1 **Why did Master Mousehasso's sentence seem familiar to Geronimo?**

Mousehasso said that in the past he had to exchange his paintings for bread and cheese. When Hercule gave Geronimo the bad painting, he told him he'd gotten it for bread and cheese. Hercule must have gotten it from Mousehasso!

2 **What did Hercule Poirat notice about the two paintings?**

The initials of the signatures on the two paintings are identical: *P.M.* and *Pablo Mousehasso*.

3 **Try to solve the anagram. What sentence do you get?**

The sentence is *Buy the black letters*.

4 **What did Benjamin see in the painting?**

He saw a black letter in the white signature.

5 **Did you recognize the place drawn on the map?**

It is Pablo Mousehasso's villa!

6 **How was Benjamin able to open the door to the secret passage?**

Benjamin pushed the numbered bricks in the sequence of the eight numbers on the canvas.

HOW MANY QUESTIONS DID YOU ANSWER CORRECTLY?

ALL 5 CORRECT: You are a **SUPER-SQUEAKY INVESTIGATOR!**

FROM 2 TO 4 CORRECT: You are a **SUPER INVESTIGATOR!** You'll get that added squeak soon!

LESS THAN 2 CORRECT: You are a **GOOD INVESTIGATOR!** Keep practicing to get super-squeaky!

Farewell until the next mystery!

Geronimo Stilton

Check out all my mini mysteries!

Don't miss any of my other fabumouse adventures!

#1 Lost Treasure of the Emerald Eye

#2 The Curse of the Cheese Pyramid

#3 Cat and Mouse in a Haunted House

#4 I'm Too Fond of My Fur!

#5 Four Mice Deep in the Jungle

#6 Paws Off, Cheddarface!

#7 Red Pizzas for a Blue Count

#8 Attack of the Bandit Cats

#9 A Fabumouse Vacation for Geronimo

#10 All Because of a Cup of Coffee

#11 It's Halloween, You 'Fraidy Mouse!

#12 Merry Christmas, Geronimo!

#13 The Phantom of the Subway

#14 The Temple of the Ruby of Fire

#15 The Mona Mousa Code

#16 A Cheese-Colored Camper

#17 Watch Your Whiskers, Stilton!

#18 Shipwreck on the Pirate Islands

#19 My Name Is Stilton, Geronimo Stilton

#20 Surf's Up, Geronimo!

#21 The Wild, Wild West

#22 The Secret of Cacklefur Castle

A Christmas Tale

#23 Valentine's Day Disaster

#24 Field Trip to Niagara Falls

#25 The Search for Sunken Treasure

#26 The Mummy with No Name

#27 The Christmas Toy Factory

#28 Wedding Crasher

#29 Down and Out Down Under

#30 The Mouse Island Marathon

#31 The Mysterious Cheese Thief

Christmas Catastrophe

#32 Valley of the Giant Skeletons

#33 Geronimo and the Gold Medal Mystery

#34 Geronimo Stilton, Secret Agent

#35 A Very Merry Christmas

#36 Geronimo's Valentine

#37 The Race Across America

#38 A Fabumouse School Adventure

#39 Singing Sensation

#40 The Karate Mouse

#41 Mighty Mount Kilimanjaro

#42 The Peculiar Pumpkin Thief

#43 I'm Not a Supermouse!

#44 The Giant Diamond Robbery

#45 Save the White Whale!

#46 The Haunted Castle

#47 Run for the Hills, Geronimo!

#48 The Mystery in Venice

#49 The Way of the Samurai

#50 This Hotel Is Haunted!

#51 The Enormouse Pearl Heist

Don't miss these very special editions!

THE KINGDOM OF FANTASY

THE QUEST FOR PARADISE: THE RETURN TO THE KINGDOM OF FANTASY

THE AMAZING VOYAGE: THE THIRD ADVENTURE IN THE KINGDOM OF FANTASY

THE DRAGON PROPHECY: THE FOURTH ADVENTURE IN THE KINGDOM OF FANTASY

ABOUT THE AUTHOR

 Born in New Mouse City, Mouse Island, **GERONIMO STILTON** is Rattus Emeritus of Mousomorphic Literature and of Neo-Ratonic Comparative Philosophy. For the past twenty years, he has been running *The Rodent's Gazette*, New Mouse City's most widely read daily newspaper.

Stilton was awarded the Ratitzer Prize for his scoops on *The Curse of the Cheese Pyramid* and *The Search for Sunken Treasure*. He has also received the Andersen 2000 Prize for Personality of the Year. One of his bestsellers won the 2002 eBook Award for world's best ratlings' electronic book. His works have been published all over the globe.

In his spare time, Mr. Stilton collects antique cheese rinds and plays golf. But what he most enjoys is telling stories to his nephew Benjamin.

1. Main entrance
2. Printing presses (where the books and newspaper are printed)
3. Accounts department
4. Editorial room (where the editors, illustrators, and designers work)
5. Geronimo Stilton's office
6. Helicopter landing pad

THE RODENT'S GAZETTE

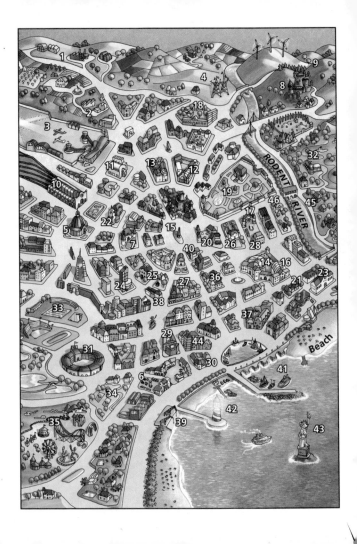